For Courtney. My world is more cheerful with you by my side.

"A good cheerleader is not measured by the height of her jumps, but by the span of her spirit"- Georgetta "Georgie" Blackburn.

Courtney could not wait to get home from church on this crisp and cold Sunday morning in December.

Ever since she was a little girl, Courtney wanted to be a Courthouse Cavalier cheerleader!

She is excited because today she is registering for her first cheerleading try-out with her two best friends, Christy and Cathy.

Courtney and her parents crept carefully through the ice and snow surrounding their Chrysler in the parking lot.

The family started their drive down Canal Street. The roads were icy and slick and cars were pumping their brakes every few minutes.

Courtney was calmly watching a video on her iPad, when suddenly she felt a jolt and heard a loud CRASH!

CANAL ST.

A Chevy truck had slammed into the side of the Conner's family vehicle, and Courtney's ankle was crunched between the car door and the back of her mom's seat.

"Is everyone alright?" asked Mr. Conner.

"My ankle is stuck!" cried Courtney.
"My cheerleading career is over," she sobbed.

The man from the Chevy truck came over and said the police were on their way.

"I was trying to avoid hitting a cocker spaniel when I lost control of my truck," he explained.

After a police incident report and a follow up to the
local urgent care, Courtney was able to hobble out
of the medical clinic with a new set of crutches.

The doctor informed Courtney she had a major sprain and would be healed up in a couple weeks.

"L-E-T-S-G-O, let's go, let's go!" her mother cheered.

Her mother was trying to keep her spirit up.

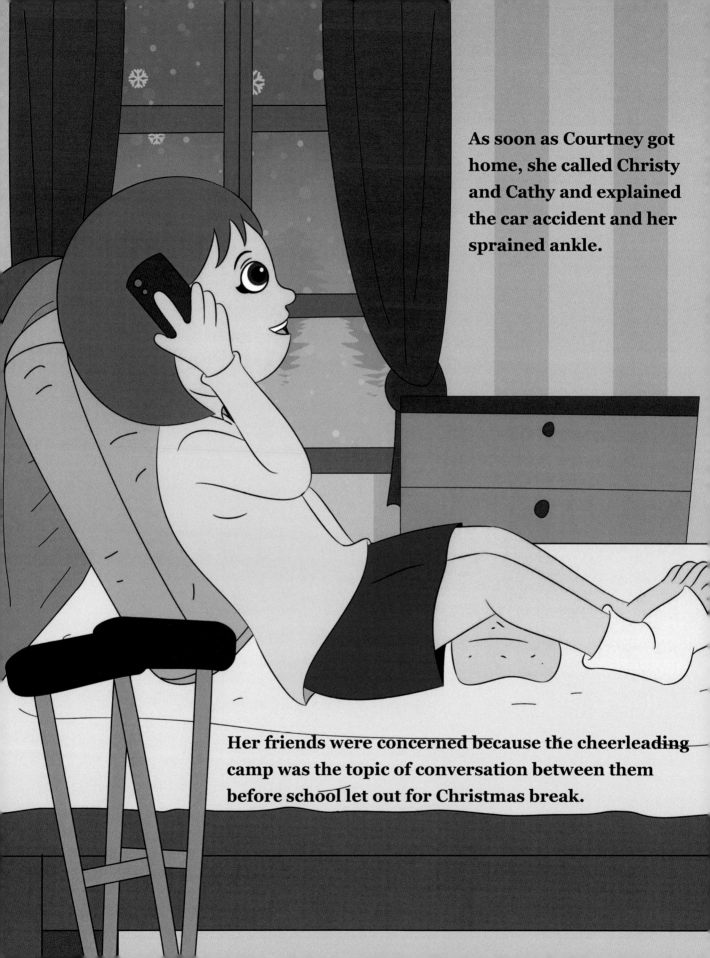

As soon as Courtney got home, she called Christy and Cathy and explained the car accident and her sprained ankle.

Her friends were concerned because the cheerleading camp was the topic of conversation between them before school let out for Christmas break.

"Never fear!" replied Cathy.

"Gather all your arts and crafts, and we will be over in a second," Christy added over Cathy's ear.

The girls worked hard and fast, and used every item on the crafting table. Glitter, spray paint, and markers in red and white stripes all around the crutches made them appear as candy canes.

"This is perfect for the holidays!" Christy remarked.

Pine needles were glued on last to complete the Christmas theme. Courtney was thrilled with her newly designed crutches! Her friends gave her the confidence she needed to change her attitude.

"Be aggressive, B-E Aggressive!" the girls cheered loudly.

The girls piled into Mr. Conner's Cadillac, as the Chrysler needed repairs, and made their way to the school safely.

Her mother and friends waited in line to gather all the paperwork needed to register.

Courtney took a seat by the hot chocolate stand, complimentary of the academic staff.

"There are a lot of kids registering," she thought out loud.

After all forms were completed, the upfront and personal interviews proceeded. Courtney was extremely nervous; however, she carried her head high and crutched over to the three-person panel composed of the coaching staff.

Courtney displayed courage as she explained her recent car accident to the committee.

"You are a compelling candidate," said the head coach. "The most important factor is the health and safety of our cheerleaders."

After Courtney's mom took Christy and Cathy home, she had Courtney elevate her leg on a pillow to help in the healing process.

Courtney started to get a game plan together by typing notes on her iPad.

The next couple of days, she confined herself to the family room couch. She kept a calender by her side and checked off the days as Christmas break came to an end. School would be back in session tomorrow, which meant the cheerleading camp try-outs would also commence.

Monday arrived and Courtney was back in the swing of things at Courthouse Middle School. Her colorful Christmas crutches were a big hit too!

The final bell rang at three o'clock and Courtney was eager to meet up with her friends in the Cavalier gymnasium. All of the potential candidates and coaches were filing in and setting up for the try-outs.

Courtney placed her crutches on the bleachers and stepped into formation. After thirty minutes of repetition, it was her turn to perform for the coaches.

There were echoes of clapping and chanting from the other competitors. These actions forced Courtney to focus on her arm placements and kept her mind off her ankle when she completed her straddle jump.

Next came the dance and tumbling portion of the try-outs. Courtney is an elite gymnast in her community; however, she had not competed during her recovery.

The only required skill each cheerleader needed to master was a back-handspring. Courtney could do that with her eyes closed.

"Nailed it!" Courtney said under her breath as she tumbled past the coaches. She added a back somersault tuck for extra points.

After the last candidate completed her skills, the coaching staff approached the bleachers where everyone who had finished was seated.

"Great job today from all of you!" the head coach announced.

"If you are selected, there will be a uniform hanging in your locker on Friday," the assistant coach remarked.

Friday morning was finally here for Courtney and her friends. The three girls quickly entered the school and ran to their lockers.

"On the count of three," Christy indicated, "One, two, three!"

The girls screamed at the top of their lungs, "WE MADE THE SQUAD!"

Students passing by gave them high fives and congrats.

Courtney had the biggest smile on her face throughout the day and couldn't wait to get home to share the news with her parents.

"The determination and motivation you exhibited during the try-outs is exactly what we want on our squad," the head coach mentioned as Courtney passed her in the hallway on her way out the doors.

"See you in the spring," Courtney shouted as she left the school grounds and headed home.

ABOUT THE AUTHOR

Jessica Marie West resides in Virginia Beach, Virginia with her significant companion, Dentron, and her three boys. She works as a Clinical Laboratory Scientist at an Organ Procurement Organization and Tissue Banking Facility.

Jessica was an avid cheerleader growing up. She cheered for her community football team until she was in high school. She was a Junior Varsity cheerleader and a Varsity Team Captain; as well, a Varsity gymnast in high school. She was also selected to cheer in the Nokia Sugar Bowl in 1996 through her high school squad. Jessica was also a cheerleader when she attended Montclair State University in Upper Montclair, New Jersey during her Sophomore year.

She is passionate about watching college cheer and gymnastics meets on ESPN.

Check out her other published works in the Alliterative Alphabet Series, "Adventurous Abbey and the Amazing Hot Air Balloon" and "Brayden's Birthday at the Ballpark" (written in English and Spanish) available on Amazon.com.

ABOUT THE ILLUSTRATORS

Sudipta Basu and Avijit Roy, commonly known as Scribbleline, are professional children's books illustrators and Vector Illustration Artists from Kolkata, West Bengal India. They studied at the Indian College of Arts and Draftsmanship and also attended Banamalipur Priyanath Institution. They are also freelance graphic designers, according to Fiverr.com, and received Bachelors of Fine Arts from Rabindra Bharati University in 2014 and BFA Certifications in 2015. They currently have skills in the following categories: hand and digital drawings, vector and raster illustrations, caricatures, and vector tracings. They also have a drawing channel on You Tube called "Drawing Ka Fanda" specifically designed for kids.

Made in the USA
Columbia, SC
03 January 2021